The Alden Family Mysteries
by Gertrude Chandler Warner

THE BOXCAR CHILDREN
SURPRISE ISLAND
THE YELLOW HOUSE MYSTERY
MYSTERY RANCH
MIKE'S MYSTERY
BLUE BAY MYSTERY
THE WOODSHED MYSTERY
THE LIGHTHOUSE MYSTERY
MOUNTAIN TOP MYSTERY
SCHOOLHOUSE MYSTERY
CABOOSE MYSTERY
HOUSEBOAT MYSTERY
SNOWBOUND MYSTERY
TREE HOUSE MYSTERY
BICYCLE MYSTERY
MYSTERY IN THE SAND
MYSTERY BEHIND THE WALL
BUS STATION MYSTERY
BENNY UNCOVERS A MYSTERY

The Woodshed Mystery

THE

WOODSHED MYSTERY

Gertrude Chandler Warner

Illustrations: David Cunningham

ALBERT WHITMAN & Company Chicago

ISBN 0-8075-9207-2

Published simultaneously in Canada by General Publishing, Limited, Toronto.

5 7 9 10 8 6

Printed in the U.S.A.

To all readers everywhere,
including Guam, who have written to me
about the Boxcar Children,
this new mystery is dedicated.

Contents

The Woodshed Mystery

CHAPTER 1

A Farm for Sale

The telephone gave a long, loud ring. Supper was over. Benny Alden was going through the hall. He answered it.

"Telephone, Grandfather!" shouted Benny. "It's for you. Long distance."

Mr. Alden came to the telephone and said, "Hello. Oh, yes."

Then he said nothing for a long, long time. Benny and his sister Violet couldn't help listening.

At last Grandfather said, "That's just fine, Jane!"

"It's Aunt Jane!" Violet whispered to Benny.

Benny nodded, and a smile spread over his face.

"Just wonderful, Jane," said Grandfather again. "Yes, I do. Yes, I think it is a fine idea. Yes, Jane. I'll think it over and call you very soon. No, Jane, I won't be long, maybe a day or two. Yes, I know you like to do things fast. You are like Benny." Grandfather winked at Benny.

At last Grandfather said, "Good-by, Jane. See you soon."

"See you soon?" said Benny. "Are we going out West to see Aunt Jane again?"

"No, she is coming here," said Mr. Alden.

"Oh, my, my!" said Benny.

"Yes, that's what I say too," said Grandfather. "Oh, my, my, my! Now you four children get together and we'll talk this over. Benny, you find Henry."

"And I'll get Jessie," said Violet. "She is up in her room."

The four Aldens—two girls and two boys—lived with their grandfather in a big house. Henry was in college. Jessie was a senior in high school, and Violet was just ready for high school, too. Benny still went to grade school. In a few minutes the four young Aldens were sitting with Mr. Alden in his den.

Grandfather looked around and smiled. "This is the big news," he said, laughing. "Aunt Jane wants to come East to live in New England again. She wants me to buy a farm for her, right away quick."

"Quick like a fox," said Benny.

"Right," said Grandfather. He laughed again.

"Why does she want to move?" asked Jessie. "She has such an exciting place to live on Mystery Ranch."

"Well, you see Jane and I were born in New England on a farm," said Mr. Alden. "We all moved to the West. I should say Jane was about eighteen when we went. I was younger than Jane. After awhile I wanted to come back and go into business. But Jane wouldn't. She said she would stay and run the ranch alone."

"Stubborn," said Benny.

"I remember," said Jessie. "That is what made the trouble between you and Aunt Jane."

"Yes, she was too proud to give in. She found she couldn't run the ranch alone. So she almost starved to death."

"Wasn't it lucky we went out there when she was sick?" said Violet. "We found such a lovely aunt."

"Well, yes—she is lovely now," said her grandfather, smiling. "Now I am going to surprise Jane. Maybe I can buy the very farm where we used to live! She would like that."

"Oh, wouldn't that be wonderful!" cried Jessie. "We could go up to the farm and get everything ready. Do you suppose we'll have to get chairs and tables and beds? We could get in food and make the beds. We'd love to do that."

"What fun that would be!" said Violet. Her eyes were very bright.

"When are you going to try, Grandfather?" asked Benny.

"Well, my boy, I am going to surprise you, too. I'm going to start this very minute. It's only just after supper."

Benny hugged Watch, the dog, and jumped up and down with him. Watch did not like this very well. But he loved Benny, so he did not make any fuss.

"Now just hand me that telephone, Henry," said Mr. Alden.

"Whose number are you going to call?" asked Benny. "How do you know what to call?"

"I don't," said Mr. Alden. But he made a call just the same. He called the village store.

"Nobody will be in the store as late as this," said Henry.

"Don't be too sure," said Mr. Alden. "In the old days the storekeeper lived in the store. Maybe he still does."

Sure enough, a loud voice answered. The children could hear every word.

"Hello," said Grandfather. "Are you the manager of the store?"

"Well, I guess so," came the answer. "It's my store."

"Do you know anything about the old Alden farm up on the hill?"

"Do I? Of course I know the Alden farm up on the hill! I live right here in this town."

"Yes, I know. Do you know if the farm is for sale?"

"Yes, 'tis. I must say 'tis. That farm is running down. Get it cheap. Furniture, too."

"Who is selling it?" asked Grandfather.

"Well, I guess I am. It hasn't brought me any luck. Who wants to buy it?"

"I do. I used to live there with my sister Jane when I was a boy. I am James Alden."

"Don't tell me!" said the man. "I remember Jane Alden well. And you too, I guess. Long time ago. And you want to buy that farm back?"

"Yes, I do."

"Well, I'll make you a fair price. All the land and the house and the barn and the hen-coops and the

woodshed. Some furniture, too. Glad to get rid of it."

"I'll buy it," said Grandfather.

"*What?*" cried the man.

"We can settle on the price when I see you," said Grandfather again. "By the way, tell me your full name."

"Well, my name is Elisha Morse. But I'm so surprised I don't know my own name for sure. You coming here to *live?*"

"No, but my sister Jane is."

"Well, well, well! This telephone call is costing you a lot of money. Better hang up."

"All right," said Grandfather. "We'll be driving up soon to see my new farm."

"It ain't new. It's old," said the man.

"It's new to me. I just bought it," said Grandfather. "Good-by and thank you."

Grandfather leaned back and laughed. He hung up the telephone. "Quick like a fox, Benny?" he said. "Is that what you wanted?"

"Grandfather, you are simply wonderful," said Benny.

"Well, I had a bit of luck, I should say," said Mr. Alden.

Everyone agreed. But it was Jessie, not Grandfather, who began to make plans right away.

CHAPTER 2

Making Plans

"What day is this?" said Jessie. "Friday. Couldn't we go tomorrow and see the place, Grandfather?"

"That is just what I was thinking," said Mr. Alden. "We could stay all day Sunday and get back for the last week of school. Of course Henry is home for the summer already."

Violet said, "I think you are the very kindest man in the world!" She took his hand in both of hers. "You spend all your time trying to make us happy."

"Well, well. Thank you, my dear. But you children spend all your time making me happy, too."

"Oh, let's talk about the farm, Grandfather," said Benny. "Do they have animals?"

"What do you think, Benny?" asked Jessie. "Nobody lives there. I don't think Aunt Jane wants any animals. She just wants to come East."

Henry nodded at his sister. "I think Aunt Jane wants to be near you, Grandfather. I think she feels safer."

"Maybe you are right, Henry," said Mr. Alden. He laughed again. "Maggie is coming with Jane. Remember Maggie who has stayed with her for so long? Then Sam and his wife will come and stay this summer anyway. And I am sure Jane will bring her dog Lady."

"That's good," said Jessie. "Maggie knows what Aunt Jane needs. They will all take care of Aunt Jane. She ought to have a man in the house."

"Yes, and Sam is a very good man," said Mr. Alden. "I don't think Jane will run the farm. But she wants

to live there. I'd like to start early tomorrow morning. Do you think you could be ready, Benny?"

"Me?" cried Benny. He went over to his grandfather and put his hand on his knee. "I'll get up any time you say. Three o'clock in the morning. Or two, or four, or even midnight! Any old time."

"How about five?" said Mr. Alden looking at Benny.

"Fine," said Benny. "Don't we have to take a bag if we stay overnight?"

"Yes, each of you must take a bag. We won't stay at the farmhouse. But we can find a motel, maybe."

"A motel!" said Benny. "That's neat."

"Let's go and pack, Jessie," said Violet. "I can hardly wait to see Aunt Jane."

"Aunt Jane won't be there," said Mr. Alden.

"No, I know that," said Violet. "But I'd like to hurry and get ready for her."

"We all seem to be in a great hurry," said Benny. "Will Aunt Jane fly?"

"Yes, I think John Carter can go out for her. Then she will not worry about a thing."

"Oh, you mean our nice Mr. Carter!" cried Jessie. "He can do anything. Aunt Jane will be safe with him."

Jessie was right. John Carter was trusted with many things by Grandfather. He even flew Mr. Alden's private plane.

"Now I think I'll go and pack my own bag," said Grandfather, getting out of his chair. "Good-night, everybody."

"Good-night?" shouted Benny. "It's only half past seven. Are we going to *bed?*"

Everybody laughed at Benny's surprised look.

"I am," said Grandfather, "and you'd better. Just pack your things first. Remember we start at five. And that means breakfast before five."

"Can we take Watch?" asked Benny.

"Yes, take Watch. It won't be a long trip."

The Aldens had the same suitcases they had taken to Blue Bay. They all knew how to pack very well. It did not take long to decide to take plain clothes. They knew they would need them on a farm.

"We won't dress up at all," said Jessie. "Just take shorts and slacks and flat shoes."

"We always take flat shoes," said Henry. "Everywhere we go we take flat shoes."

"Oh, Henry, don't tease," laughed Jessie. "I know boys do."

When four o'clock in the morning came, Benny was fast asleep. He did not hear the alarm clock. Violet went into his room and shook him gently.

"No," said Benny. "No! It isn't morning yet. It's too dark."

"You said you'd get up at midnight or four o'clock. Any old time," said Violet.

"It's different now," said Benny.

Violet laughed. She put on all the lights and Benny got out of bed.

The family ate a big breakfast of bacon and eggs, cereal and toast and orange juice. Then they all piled into the big station wagon. Henry drove. It was a beautiful spring day. The woods were just beginning to look green. The fields were covered with dandelions. Birds sang in the trees as the sun came up. The family went along the smooth turnpike on the way north.

"We should get there by nine o'clock," said Grandfather. "I'll tell you where to turn, Henry."

A little later he shouted, "Here we are, Henry! Turn here! See the white church over there? And that other building is the town hall. And there is the old store! How small it looks! It used to look big."

They were delighted to find the store so easily. Everyone got out of the car and went into the store.

"My gracious me!" said the man behind the counter. "I bet you're James Alden. I'm Elisha Morse."

"I remember your name, Elisha," said Grandfather. He shook hands.

For several minutes the two men talked about the sale of the farm. Then Mr. Alden wrote out a check and gave it to Mr. Morse.

"I don't think you're going to like your farm," Mr. Morse said as he put the check away. "The roof leaks."

"Can't it be fixed?" asked Mr. Alden.

"Sure. Only it will cost money. I'd do it for you if I had the money."

"Would you fix it yourself?"

"No. My son is the handy one. He could put on new shingles."

"You get him if you can," said Grandfather. "We'll go right up to the house. Ask your son to come up and see me. We must certainly have the roof fixed."

"Good," said Mr. Morse. "Here's the key to the back door. My son will come in soon to see who was in the store."

Mr. Morse came out and watched the Aldens get back into the station wagon. He said nothing. The car began to move. Still Mr. Morse said nothing. But when the car had rolled down the drive, he called, "There's a lot of other things the matter with that farm! You won't like it!"

But the Aldens were on their way to the farm on the hill and Henry did not turn back.

CHAPTER 3

Grandfather Takes Over

"Now why in the world did Mr. Morse call to us after I got started?" asked Henry.

"Well, that's the way people are up here," said Grandfather. "I remember now. You have to get used to it. They have all the time there is. Never in a hurry."

"I suppose I should have gone back." said Henry.

"No," said Grandfather. "We'll wait now and see the house. Then we will find out what's wrong. These people are the best people in the world. They will do anything for you. You just wait and see. They can even hurry if you tell them why."

Violet looked at Jessie and smiled. They loved to see their grandfather so happy. He was looking all around him at the little village.

"See!" he said. "There's the old Bean farm!"

"Bean farm?" said Benny. "Do they raise beans?"

"Oh, no. Mr. and Mrs. Bean used to live there. They had two sons," said Mr. Alden. "I remember the Bean boy who was just about my age. In mischief all the time. Good looking boy, but always in trouble." Mr. Alden threw his head back and laughed. "I remember Jane liked him pretty well. Very well, I mean. She always stood up for him."

"What became of him?" asked Benny. "Did he grow up bad?"

"I don't know, Benny. That's a long story. You see he got into trouble with an old gun up here. The next day he was gone. Nobody ever found him. Jane felt pretty bad. I think Jane might have married him."

"He ran away?" asked Henry.

"Yes, I suppose he did. Later on, we heard he ran away to sea. He got a job on a ship and went around the world. Anyway, nobody knows where he is now. He may be dead. Probably is dead."

"Aunt Jane would be sorry," said Violet.

Mr. Alden looked at his gentle granddaughter. "Yes, Jane would be sorry. Nobody ever knew where he got that gun."

"Did he shoot anybody with it?" asked Benny.

"No. He shot at the big trees to scare people. Queer thing happened. He started a forest fire. Oh, what a fire that was! The house almost caught on fire. But the neighbors put it out. In the morning he was gone."

"What was his first name?" asked Jessie.

"Now what was his name?" said Grandfather. "I have forgotten. It was a long time ago. I was a boy myself."

"It's a nice house," said Henry.

"Yes, but not as nice as our farmhouse. Ours was

built in 1750. There are four big chimneys. You can see the date on the front chimney, I think. It used to be there. There! Look over there! That's the old house!"

Mr. Alden was so excited that the children were excited too. They looked toward the top of the hill. There stood an enormous white farmhouse. Two large elm trees stood beside the house. Behind the house was a great red barn, and behind the barn was a field and then woods.

"I don't see anything bad about the house," said Jessie. "It needs paint, maybe. But it looks all right to me."

"The roof leaks," said Benny.

"Wait and see," said Henry. "I think that if Mr. Morse said we wouldn't like it, something must be wrong with it."

"There's the 1750 on the chimney," cried Benny. "Painted white."

Henry turned the station wagon again and there they were, right by the back door of the house. They all got out of the car. They stood and looked at the house. Then Henry put the big key in the back door and turned it.

"The door key works anyway," he said. He pushed the door open.

"I'll go in first," said Mr. Alden. "Then you children follow. Nobody has been here for a long time." The house looked cool and dim inside.

First they found themselves in a back pantry. Next came the old kitchen.

"Oh, look!" cried Jessie. "What an enormous fireplace!"

"I could lie down in that fireplace!" shouted Benny.

"Don't," said Jessie. "And look at the old brick ovens on both sides." She opened the doors.

"Say!" exclaimed Benny. "That must be where they baked bread."

The kitchen was a big room. Next everyone went into the sitting room. The carpet was dusty, but not too worn. The chairs and tables were covered with dust.

The Aldens turned to the left and came to the long hall. The front door was at one end of the hall. On the other side of the hall was a parlor and a bedroom. The Aldens walked quickly through these rooms. There would be time to explore them later.

"I suppose there are four bedrooms upstairs," said Jessie.

"Oh, let's go upstairs," said Benny. "Maybe there is something wrong up there."

"I can't see anything wrong downstairs," said Henry. "It's only dirty and dusty. A fireplace in every room. Think of that!"

"Upstairs, too," said Grandfather. "That's how we kept warm. There were no heaters in those days."

Upstairs they went. There were the four bedrooms. No bathroom.

"We simply can't stay here, Grandfather," said Jessie, the good housekeeper. "It is too dirty."

"Oh, no! We will stay at a motel as I said. Maybe we can get somebody to clean this place up."

"We could do it," said Benny.

"No, it will take a strong woman to do this. And maybe a man would be still better," said Mr. Alden. He looked around thoughtfully.

"There's a man at the back door," said Benny. "I can see his car."

They all went down to find a tall young man getting out of a car.

"Are you Mr. Morse's son who can fix the roof?" asked Benny.

"That's right, son," said the man. "Call me Sim. I'm Simeon Morse."

"Oh, that'll be neat!" shouted Benny. "When Sam comes we'll have Sim and Sam!"

"And who is Sam?" asked Sim.

"He is coming with my sister," said Mr. Alden. "You'll get along fine with Sam. He and his wife are going to handle the farm work for my sister. Now I want you to tell me the truth, young man. *What* is the matter with this house?"

Sim stood on one foot and then the other. He was very nervous.

"Well, I'll tell you the truth. I *don't* know."

"You don't know? Then what makes you think there is any trouble here?"

"I don't know that, either," said Sim.

Grandfather sat down in a kitchen chair and leaned forward. "Now, Simeon," he said. "You sit right down here. I want to know just what's going on.

Your father says there is something strange about this place. And you think so, too. What makes you think so? After all, I used to live here and nothing seemed so mysterious then."

Sim looked at Grandfather for a moment. Then he said, "But your family left, just the way all the others have. Nobody stays."

"But what is it that makes you think this?" Grandfather asked.

"Kind of silly," said Sim.

"Never mind that. I want to know what it is, silly or not."

"Well," said Sim, "maybe you know the Bean family? Used to live over in that next house?"

"I certainly do."

Sim went on. "There used to be an older boy there who found a gun some place."

"I know," said Grandfather. "I have forgotten his first name."

"Andrew," said Sim.

"That's right! Andrew it was! We called him

Andy and his father didn't like it. Andy Bean! How could I forget that? Now what's the story?"

"Well, that Andrew was wild. He made a lot of trouble. And that gun set this whole place on fire. They put the fire out, but Andrew never showed up again. *Never*. His brother got the farm."

"Well, what's the matter with this house? That was long ago."

Sim looked at Mr. Alden. "You want the truth of it? Seems as if nobody ever got along very well here after that. Bad to worse. People tell all kinds of stories. They *say* that Andrew found the gun here, and somebody was hiding here and gave it to him. Somebody up to no good."

"Now who could that be?"

"I don't know. It was a terrible long time ago."

"What kind of a gun was it?" asked Henry.

"Yes! That's a good question. We've got that gun over to my father's house right now. It's an awful old gun. The kind they used in the Revolutionary War. Long time ago."

"I should like to see that gun very much," said Mr. Alden.

"See it any time," said Sim. "Ask my father."

Mr. Alden looked at Henry and Jessie. "I think there is some story about this gun. And we need to find out what it is!"

"Oh, boy!" cried Benny. "And now we'll have some fun. When my grandfather really gets going, Sim, things *happen*."

"I bet," said Sim. He smiled at Benny.

"Now, Sim," Mr. Alden went on, "is this house dangerous? Can't it be fixed and cleaned up?"

"Sure," said Sim. "Nothing wrong with the house itself, I guess." He scowled.

"I thought you said there *was* something wrong with the house!" cried Mr. Alden.

"It's just what people say and how they feel about this place. Bad luck. The *house* is all right. I guess we ought to put a heavy post in the cellar to make the floor safe. Fix the roof. Fix the windows. Paint a little. You could live here OK."

"Well, you're a fine friend," said Mr. Alden. "I'm glad we found you. Can you get some help and start right to work on this place? Today?"

"Today? Well, I don't know about today."

"Why not?" asked Grandfather. "Are you busy somewhere else?"

"Well, I guess I could leave. I'm just fixing my tractor. Do that any time."

"What about help?"

"I guess the neighbors would help. They are glad Miss Alden is coming back here. May change the old place's luck."

"You mean the neighbors know already?" asked Grandfather.

"Oh, sure. Knew that last night. Everybody knew it last night."

"Well, news goes around fast," said Grandfather. He laughed. "I remember it did when I lived here. You get your help because I don't know the people yet. Start right away. I will give you some money to buy paint, wood, and that beam for the cellar." He counted out some money for Sim to use.

"You folks can't live here now," said Sim, looking at the four children.

"Oh, no. We thought we could find a motel."

"Yes, you can. Right down the road, about four miles. It's a nice motel. Got a carpet on the floor and a TV and everything."

"Oh, Sim," said Jessie, "how about a bathroom in this house? Can you put in a bathroom?"

"Where did you want a bathroom?" asked Sim.

"I thought two," said Jessie. "You could easily take a piece of the big hall. One upstairs and one downstairs."

"Right, Jessie," said her grandfather. "Anybody around here put in a bathroom?"

Sim scratched his head. "I always wanted to put in a bathroom," he said. "Costs too much, though."

"Well, you go ahead," said Mr. Alden. "Get all the men you need. The thing is, I want this done as soon as possible. Jane wants to move right away this minute."

"She's changed some, I guess," said Sim. "My father says she used to move slow. And you were the fast one."

"Right," said Mr. Alden. "Jane has changed a lot. We both move fast now, Sim. Tell your father."

"No fear," said Sim. "I tell him everything."

While Mr. Alden and Sim talked, Violet and Benny went exploring.

Violet found a path through the uncut grass of the yard. It led to the front door. There she found some big, flat flagstones, warm in the sun.

Benny ran toward the barn. He poked his head through the crack left by a sagging door. The barn was dark and empty. An old lantern hung on a peg beside a broken harness. Nothing moved. "Spooky," Benny thought to himself.

Suddenly it seemed a long time since their early breakfast. Benny ran back to Grandfather. "I'm hungry," he said.

"Again?" asked Grandfather. "Have you forgotten that breakfast?"

"I have myself, Grandfather," said Violet. "I wish we could have a picnic and not go to the motel for lunch. This is such a nice yard."

"You call this a nice yard?" asked Sim. "You ought to see it when the grass is cut. Looks good."

"Look at those enormous flat stones by the front door," said Violet. We could take a chair out there for Grandfather and have a fine picnic."

Mr. Alden always listened to Violet. "Well," he said, "let's go down to the motel and get some sandwiches, and ask them to fill our Thermos bottles. Could we get sandwiches at the motel, Sim?"

"Well, you could," said Sim. "But my wife would love to make you some chicken sandwiches. She makes 'em fine."

"Neat!" cried Benny.

"Could make some egg sandwiches, too," said Sim.

"We'll be right down," cried Benny.

"I'll go down and tell her," said Sim. "And I'll call up some of the neighbors and tell them about this job."

"Ah!" said Grandfather. His eyes were shining.

"Ah!" said Benny. For a minute he looked just like his grandfather. Sim looked at them both. He saw how much they wanted the house fixed. He said to himself, "They want that house fixed quick, and it will be fixed quick."

CHAPTER 4

The Potato Pit

"You go on ahead, Sim," said Mr. Alden. "We'll follow if you are sure your wife wants to make sandwiches for us."

"Yes, I'm sure," said Sim. "We got lots of milk, too. We can fill up your Thermos bottles."

"We'll drink more milk than that, Sim," said Henry. "There are four of us, you know. I could drink a quart myself right now."

"Let's have one Thermos of coffee for Grandfather," said Violet, who always thought of Grandfather.

"You can have all the milk you want," said Sim. "We have forty cows."

They all went out the back door.

"Don't lock the door," said Sim. "Just leave it."

He got into his car. The family got into the station wagon and off they went. This time they went to the red house nearest the store. Sim took them into the kitchen. His wife smiled when she saw them coming.

"Ma, can you make some chicken sandwiches? This is Mr. Alden and his grandchildren. They want a picnic lunch."

"How do you do, Mrs. Morse," said Grandfather, shaking hands. "You are very kind to do this for us."

"Glad to," said Mrs. Morse. "I made bread yesterday so I have six loaves."

"Oh, homemade bread!" said Benny. "What a picnic!"

"Make some egg sandwiches too, Ma," said Sim.

"These children seem to be half starved. I'll get the cans of milk."

"Why do you call her ma?" asked Benny. "Isn't she your wife?"

"Yes, she's my wife. But I call her ma because we have six kids."

Mrs. Morse began to chop up chicken in a wooden tray. "You have courage," she said, "to move into that old house."

"Why?" asked Benny. "It isn't *haunted*, is it?"

"No, it isn't haunted," said Mrs. Morse. "But nobody in this town would live in it."

"Why not?" asked Grandfather. "I'd really like to know."

"Well, I can't tell you why. But there is something mysterious about it. I never did know what it was."

"That's the funniest thing!" said Jessie. "Nobody seems to know."

"Did something happen a long time ago?" asked Henry.

Mrs. Morse looked up. "Yes, that's exactly right!

It happened so long ago, nobody remembers. But they remember there was *something*."

"Who is the oldest person in this town?" Henry asked.

"Oldest person? Let me think. That would be Grandpa Cole. He's almost a hundred years old. But he can still see to read and he can walk with a cane."

"Maybe he would remember something he heard when he was a boy," said Jessie.

"Maybe he would. That's right. I never asked Grandpa Cole," said Mrs. Morse. She began to crack eggs and take off the shells.

Benny's eyes grew wide with surprise.

"Oh, those eggs were hard-boiled already!" cried Benny. "I thought they would run out when I saw you crack them."

"Yes, I always have cold eggs for my family. They like cold hard-boiled eggs for breakfast."

"Well, I don't," said Benny. "I like cold eggs for a picnic. And for breakfast I like them hot and soft-boiled."

Mrs. Morse laughed. "Most people do," she said. "I've got a funny family."

She was an excellent cook, though. Soon she took out a big basket with a handle. She began to wrap the sandwiches in waxed paper. She put them in the basket. "You like pickles?" she asked.

"Oh, we love pickles!" said Benny. He looked up. He expected to see a bottle of pickles. But these pickles were as long as his hand.

"My, those are superman pickles," he said. "One will be enough. It looks just like a cucumber."

"Pickles are cucumbers, Benny," said Jessie.

"Well, I never knew that," said Benny.

"I have some cookies, too," said Mrs. Morse. "You'd better have some cookies for dessert."

They were big round white cookies with a hole in the middle. They were brown around the edges. How good they smelled!

"There you are," she said at last. She shut the cover of the basket. "Good luck!" She gave a Thermos of coffee to Jessie.

Henry took the basket and thanked her. Grandfather paid her. That is, he tried to pay her. But she gave the money right back. "No," she said, "I love to do something like that. It was a pleasure."

Mr. Alden knew she meant it. So he said he would always remember it, and each one of the four children thanked her again.

Off they went in the station wagon, back to the farm. They took the basket to the big flat stones by the front door. Henry found a chair for Grandfather. The rest sat on the warm stones. Out came the sandwiches, the eggs, the pickles.

Mrs. Morse had put in some paper cups for milk, and one beautiful cup and saucer and a spoon for Mr. Alden. "That's good!" said Grandfather. "I like my coffee in a cup."

"Not a paper cup," said Benny.

"Right. No paper cup for me."

On top of the basket was an enormous bone for Watch. He took it and went off with it. Everyone was eating cookies when they heard a car coming.

Watch began to bark. He ran right over to the children, but he wagged his tail.

"Now who is that?" asked Jessie.

"I bet it's the man to fix the roof," said Benny.

He was right. A thin man with white hair stopped his car and got out. He looked at the children and Mr. Alden. He had a load of shingles in the back of his car.

"Are you the man to fix the roof?" Benny asked.

"Yep," said the man.

"Have you got a long ladder?" asked Henry.

"Nope."

"I suppose you have to wait for Sim to bring a ladder," said Grandfather.

"Yep," said the man. He began to take the shingles out of his car.

Grandfather smiled. "Will you tell me your name?"

"Yep. It's Delbert King. But call me Del."

Benny said, "You heard my Aunt Jane wants to come here to live? Quick like a fox. How long do you think it will take to shingle this roof?"

"I don't know," said Del. He took out a big box of nails. Another car came slowly up the drive.

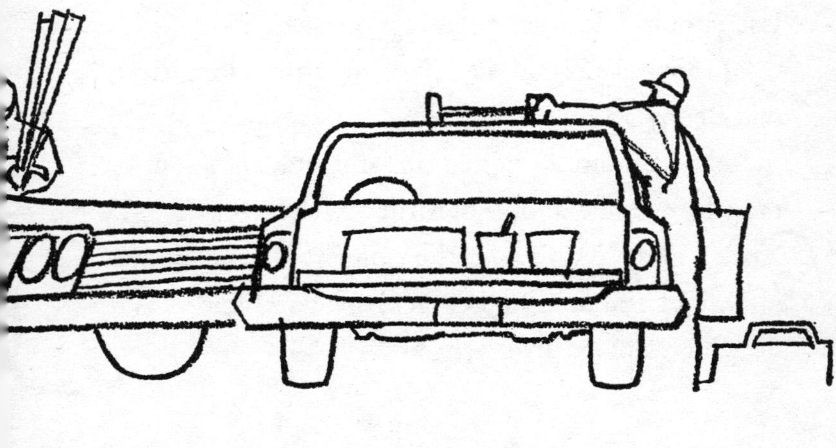

"Now who is that?" said Jessie.

"I bet it's another man to work on the house," said Henry.

"Look," said Violet. "There are three men in that car. Grandfather, you can turn a whole town upside down in no time!"

Then Sim came back too. He had another man with him. Now there were six men.

Grandfather said to Sim, "Let's go into the house and see what to do first." Everyone followed. Watch went along, wagging his tail.

The boards in the floor were very wide.

"Some of this just needs cleaning," said Sim. "The last people left it in pretty good shape."

"I thought nobody had lived here for a long time," said Benny.

"No, a family moved in and stayed about six months a while ago. Then they went back to New York. They didn't like the country," said Sim.

One of the men looked at Benny and said, "Why do you want to live here anyway?"

"We don't," said Benny. "It's my Aunt Jane. She used to live here. And Grandfather, too. This is Grandfather. He used to live here when he was a boy."

Grandfather looked at the workman. "What's the matter with the house?" he asked.

"I don't know," said the man. He stood on one foot and then the other. He looked at Sim. "Always something queer about this place. Lots of stories."

"Tell me one," said Grandfather. "Just one story."

"Well, there was an old gun."

"Yes, we've heard about that gun!" said Grandfather. "Sim has it at his house."

"No, it's at my father's house," said Sim.

"Well, I shall see it soon," said Grandfather. "What about the gun?"

"They say it came from this house," said the workman. "I guess it was a musket. It was a long time ago."

"Same story," said Grandfather. "I am going to fix up the house just the same. Fix the windows. Fix the roof. Put in bathrooms. Put in hot water. A furnace. How long will that take?"

"Well, three weeks," said Sim. "We've got a lot of men."

Violet said, "School will be out, and we can come up and stay awhile."

"We'll find out what the matter is," said Benny. "I bet it's *nothing*. Just stories people tell."

The men looked at Benny and laughed. "Maybe it's nothing, son, but I bet it's *something*."

"Well, if it is, my grandfather will find out," said Benny.

"That's the truth," said Sim. "He will."

The men went out and put ladders up to the roof. Some of the men stayed inside and began to build a fire in the stove.

"Are you cold?" asked Henry. It was a very warm day.

"No, we have to heat water from the well," said a man.

The workers had big kettles and soon there was

plenty of hot water. The men began to wash the floors and walls.

After awhile the Aldens tired of watching the work. They went down to the cellar.

"Oh, what a place!" cried Benny as his eyes grew used to the darkness. "I can believe this cellar was here during the Revolution."

"A dirt floor with rocks coming through," Henry said as he looked about. "I suppose people kept vegetables down here in the winter."

"Right, Henry," said Grandfather. "We kept potatoes in that pit. We called it the potato pit. I remember it very well. I used to come down here and get two dozen potatoes for dinner. We had so many men working on the farm then."

The four young Aldens went over the rocks to look into the hole. It was quite deep. It was lined with stones and plastered.

"No potatoes," said Benny.

They all laughed, and Violet said, "Imagine finding a potato from Revolutionary days!"

"Well," said Grandfather with a smile, "I can't say that I remember the Revolution. But we kept potatoes there. And probably that was always the place for potatoes."

"Maybe the mystery is in the potato pit," said Jessie. She looked over the edge again.

"No, I don't think so," said Mr. Alden. He started to go upstairs. "I lived here a long time. There was nothing in that pit but potatoes."

"I wonder if the mystery is in the big fireplace in the kitchen," said Violet. "Let's look in those ovens." They went upstairs to the kitchen.

"Let's get in," said Benny. It was a fine idea. Benny could get into the ovens and stand up. There was an oven on each side of the fireplace.

But not a clue was to be found.

"Well, I think we had better find that motel," said Mr. Alden. He looked at his watch. "We will have to have three rooms."

"Oh, I hope they will take dogs," said Benny. "Some motels won't take animals."

The men had finished washing the floor in the sitting room.

"Oh, how lovely this looks!" cried Jessie. "Wait till we get up some white curtains!"

The men looked at her.

"A fine job, men," said Grandfather. "When you get through, just walk out. No need to lock the door, so Sim tells me." He smiled at every man.

"That's it," said Henry to himself. "I can see why people enjoy working for Grandfather. He always looks right at them and smiles."

CHAPTER 5

An Old Flintlock Gun

The Aldens found a fine motel. The man said he would take Watch if they tied him up. Watch did not like this at all, but he lay down by the beds.

After breakfast on Sunday morning, Henry said, "The men won't be working Sunday of course. So this is just the time to go and see that old gun."

They drove back to the store. The store was shut, but Mr. Morse saw them coming. He went down to let them in.

"I bet you came to see the old gun," he said. "Come right upstairs. I live alone because my wife died many years ago."

When they were all sitting down, Mr. Morse went to a shelf and took down a queer gun.

"Well," said Benny, "that is the funniest looking gun I ever saw. Does it work? Will it shoot?"

"Oh, yes, it will shoot. But I don't know how to shoot it myself. It is called a flintlock. They used guns like this in the Revolution."

"I think I know how it works," said Henry. "Just let me take it a minute. See, here is a pan. You put the gunpowder in that pan. Then here is a flint. The flint makes a spark when you pull this trigger. That sets fire to the powder."

"I bet it makes a terrible bang," said Benny.

"Yes, it does. I have read about them. I think the one who shoots it might get hurt himself," answered Mr. Morse.

Grandfather said, "Elisha, where did you get this gun?"

"I got it from the Bean family. After Andy skipped out, they didn't want to see this gun. They were going to throw it away. So I said to give it to me. It's been on that shelf ever since. Going on fifty years! I never clean it any more."

Then Henry gave the gun to Jessie. She said, "This ought to be in a museum."

Henry said, "Now who did you say was the oldest person here? Grandpa Cole?"

"I didn't tell you about Grandpa Cole. Must have been my son."

"It was Sim's wife," said Violet. "She said he was almost a hundred years old. Where does he live?"

"Could we go and call on him?" asked Mr. Alden. He never wanted to waste words.

"Well, you could. He'd sure be surprised. Nobody ever calls on him now. He's too old. He just talks about the past," said Mr. Morse.

"Well," said Grandfather, "we want him to talk about the past."

"He will," said Mr. Morse laughing. "Go back on this road, past your own farm, and Grandpa Cole lives in the next house. A little white house with a white fence around it."

The station wagon was soon on the road again. They went past their own house with the ladders still up on the roof. Then they saw the small white house with the white fence. They all got out.

"I hope we won't scare him," said Benny. "So many strangers."

Mr. Cole was not scared. He was very much pleased. He came out in the yard and told them to sit down on the benches. A nice motherly lady came out and helped him into an easy chair.

"We won't stay very long, Mr. Cole," began Grandfather.

"Call me Grandpa," said the old man.

"Very well." Grandfather Alden smiled. "We want to ask you some questions, but we don't want to tire you."

"You won't tire me. Stay as long as you can," said Grandpa Cole. "I don't get many visitors, and I like visitors."

"That's good," said Benny. "This is very important."

"What's that?" asked Grandpa Cole. "Important? What can I tell you?"

Grandfather began again. "I know you have heard the story of the old gun that Andy Bean had."

"Yep. An old flintlock. He set a big fire with that flintlock, and then he skipped out."

"Well, this is what we want to know," said Mr. Alden leaning forward. "Where did that gun come from?"

"Where did that gun come from? Well, that's easy. It came from the farmhouse you just bought for yourself! Somebody gave it to Andy. Now that's another story. I don't know exactly who it was, but it was somebody hiding in your house!"

"Hiding? Why?" asked Benny.

"I don't know that, and I'm sure Andy's brother who has the farm doesn't know either. He wouldn't talk about it anyway. But I can tell you who does know."

"Who?" cried everybody at once.

"My brother. He is only 92 years old and I am 99.

He was younger than I was, and he would remember better."

"What is his name?" asked Henry.

"Well, Cole. Only he is John Cole and nobody calls him grandpa."

"Where is he now?" asked Jessie eagerly.

"In New York. He lives in the city in the winter. He comes up here in the summer. He'll be here in a few weeks. Maybe in a few days. I lose track of the time."

Violet said to Jessie, "Maybe he'll be here when we come up to stay. Then we can ask him. That will be after Aunt Jane comes, too."

Grandpa Cole didn't know anything more. But as Henry said, every little bit helps.

The Aldens thought Grandpa Cole was beginning to look tired. It was time to go.

"Well, thank you," said Mr. Alden. He got up and shook hands with the old man. "The children will come up soon to get the house ready for my sister Jane."

"Yes, I heard all about it," said Grandpa. "I hope she gets along all right in that house." He shook his head.

"We're going to live there too this summer," said Benny. "We're going to visit Aunt Jane."

"Come and see me," said Grandpa Cole.

As they rode back to their own farm, Mr. Alden said, "I think we might as well go home now. We can't do anything more."

"Don't you have to talk to Sim and tell the men what to do?" asked Benny.

"No, I told them already," said Grandfather.

So the family said good-by to their new friends and went back home.

In a few weeks Grandfather had a telephone call that the house was done. Jessie and Violet were ready with curtains for the windows. They had sheets and blankets and towels and lots of other things.

It took many trips to load the station wagon. And when everything was packed in, there was hardly room for Watch to ride along.

John Carter flew out to get Aunt Jane. Sam and his wife, who worked for her, had already started to drive East in their car. Maggie, however, came along with Aunt Jane.

How excited Aunt Jane was when she saw the farm where she had been born. Of course Aunt Jane was really the Alden children's great-aunt. She and Grandfather were sister and brother.

Tiny and lively, Aunt Jane moved quickly, just as her brother did. Now her cheeks were pink and her eyes danced as she looked around her new home.

"James," she cried, "you always surprise me. How did you ever get this farm back?"

"Very easily," said Grandfather. "Nobody wanted it, Jane."

"Well, I want it," said Aunt Jane. "I will be very happy here. Maggie will like it, too. And what a fine summer we will have with all the children!"

"And Watch," said Benny.

The girls and Maggie made the beds, put food in the refrigerator and new dishes in the kitchen. They brought a toaster and a coffee percolator for Mr. Alden.

Sam and his wife arrived. Sam got busy right away. He bought chickens from a neighbor. He fixed up the hen house. The farm became a busy place.

After a week Mr. Alden went back to work. But Aunt Jane, Maggie, and the four children stayed. They felt as if they had always lived on the old farm.

CHAPTER 6

Exploring the Woodshed

Soon everyone in town knew the four young Aldens. They went everywhere.

One morning Benny went over to the Bean farm. He met Mr. Bean, Andy's brother, and Mrs. Bean. They were glad to see Benny and told him to come often. But they never said a word about Andy, the older brother who had run away.

At lunch Benny said, "Here's something funny. You know the Beans raise eggs."

"They raise hens, Benny," said Jessie smiling.

"Well, anyway, they *sell* eggs. And every day about three eggs are gone."

"How do you know, old fellow? How do the Beans know?" asked Henry.

"Well, Mrs. Bean told *me*," said Benny.

Violet laughed and said, "Henny Penny told *me*."

"No, really," said Benny. "No fooling. You ought to see the list of eggs. They have a paper in the kitchen. It's on the wall. Every time they put down how many eggs they get." Everyone waited, smiling at Benny.

Benny went on. "Well, this is how the numbers go: 35 the first day, then 36, 34, 35, 35. You see—always about 35 eggs? Then one day suddenly it's like this: 32, 31, 33, 31, 30. See? Somebody's stealing eggs."

"Imagine that!" said Aunt Jane. "This is a very honest town."

"A mystery!" said Henry. "The Case of the Stolen Eggs!"

Jessie laughed at Henry's joke, but Benny was serious.

"We've been everywhere in this town except the woods," said Benny. "Let's go up to the woods to-day."

"Well, you can go if you wish," said Aunt Jane. "But these woods are not as interesting as the ranch. In the fall you can find nuts. But there is nothing there now except the brook and the old woodshed."

The boys looked interested just the same.

"Woodshed?" asked Henry. "Why did they put a woodshed so far away from the house?"

"A good question, Henry," said Aunt Jane, much pleased. "They used to cut down the enormous trees. Then they cut them up right where they fell. They used to fill that woodshed with new wood. Sometimes they left it for a year to season. The woodshed kept the snow off."

"It burns better when it's old," said Benny.

"Oh, much better. Green wood will hardly burn at all."

The day was hot. The children walked slowly up the hill to the woods.

Violet stopped to pick a few flowers. She said, "Aunt Jane loves flowers."

The Aldens knew the names of many wild flowers. Violet picked a few pink lady's-slippers, a jack-in-the-pulpit, and some white foamflowers.

"I see the old woodshed," said Benny. "It isn't much."

"No," said Jessie. "It's just a woodshed. Aunt Jane told you that."

At last they stood in front of the woodshed. They looked at it.

"No windows," said Benny. "If it had windows it would be a fine playhouse."

Henry pushed the door open. He looked in. It was dark inside. He looked again.

"This is strange," he said. "You look, Jessie."

Jessie put her head in the door.

"Somebody lives here!" she cried.

"Let me see!" shouted Benny. Then they all went inside.

"I don't see a thing," said Violet.

"Wait a minute, Violet," said Henry. "Your eyes will get used to the dark."

"A table!" cried Benny. "And a bench under it!"

It was true. A small table stood in the corner with a bench under it. On the table were two old plates, a cup, and a fork and spoon.

"No knife," said Benny. "I bet somebody has a knife right in his pocket."

"There is no food, either," said Jessie.

"Yes, there is, Jessie! Look up!" Violet was excited.

Sure enough, there was a shelf over the table. On it was a wide shingle and four cans of food. There were beef and ham and canned string beans and peas.

"What do you know!" said Henry. "We must tell Sam about this. I don't think we'd better tell Aunt Jane."

"Do you think it would scare her?" Benny asked.

"I'm afraid so," said Henry. "What do you think, Jessie?"

"I don't know. Let's tell Sam first anyway."

While they talked, Violet looked carefully around the one room.

"There must be a bed," said Violet. "I don't see one."

But Watch did. He had found the bed easily and was lying on it.

"Sometimes I think that Watch can see in the dark," said Violet. "It's just a blanket on some hay. I wonder where the hay came from?"

"Maybe from some barn," said Henry. "Plenty of hay around here."

Then they saw the egg. It was behind the cans.

"An egg!" shouted Benny. "I told you somebody was stealing eggs. This is where the eggs go! Three every day! A mystery!"

"Two mysteries," said Henry. "Who takes the eggs and who lives here?" Then he turned around suddenly. "Let's go," he said.

They all knew why Henry wanted to go. He thought the man who lived in the woodshed might come along. And he did not want Violet to feel frightened.

Violet left in such a hurry that she forgot her wild flowers on the little table.

When they reached home, they found Sam very busy indeed with his new chickens.

They lost no time in telling Sam about the woodshed and what they had found inside it. They tried to get Sam to help them guess who might be making the woodshed a home. It seemed like such an odd thing for anyone to do.

Sam looked at the Aldens and shook his head. They were always getting mixed up in something.

"I can't come now," he said. "That woodshed won't run away."

"Don't you believe us?" asked Benny. "We all saw it."

"Sure I believe you," Sam said. But he laughed. "It could be a playhouse," he said.

"Whose playhouse?" asked Benny.

"Well, any of the neighbors," said Sam. "There must be lots of children in the town."

They decided not to tell Aunt Jane. They could tell her later. They had to wait because Sam would not go until after lunch.

"Where are you all going?" Aunt Jane asked.

"We want Sam to see that woodshed!" Benny said. "It looks like Abraham Lincoln's log cabin."

Aunt Jane said nothing. But she knew something was going on. Maggie knew, too.

"It beats all, Miss Jane," said Maggie. "Those four always find such interesting things."

"So they do, Maggie. They'll tell us when they get ready."

Sam walked slowly up the hill. Benny danced on ahead with Watch.

"You'll soon see for yourself, Sam," he said.

They reached the woodshed. Benny pushed the door wide open. "Go right in, Sam, and look around."

Sam went in and stood still.

"I don't see a thing," he said.

"Wait," called Violet. "Your eyes have to get used to the dark."

But still Sam could not see anything. The four went inside and looked around.

"What! What!" cried Benny.

The woodshed was empty. There was no bed, no table, no bench, no food. Nothing at all.

"No egg," said Benny softly.

Henry looked at Sam. "But they really were here, Sam. We all saw them. You'll have to believe me."

"I do believe you," said Sam. "Now what next? What'll you do?"

Violet said, "We'll certainly have to tell Aunt Jane now."

"Yes," Henry agreed. "That's what we will do."

CHAPTER 7

Clues from an Old Book

Back at the farmhouse Henry told Aunt Jane the whole story.

"What a story that is!" she said. "But I'm not afraid with Sim and Sam here. Who do you suppose is living in my woodshed?"

"It's a good housekeeper," said Jessie. "Everything was as neat as a pin."

"Why don't you find out when Mr. Cole is coming?" said Aunt Jane. "He might know something about that woodshed. That is the next thing I'd do."

Henry went with Jessie to see Grandpa Cole. It was not a long walk.

Grandpa was sitting outdoors, reading.

"Do you know when your brother is coming?" Henry asked.

"Not till July first," said Grandpa Cole. "When New York gets hot, he comes up here. He hates to travel."

Jessie said, "We want to see him when he comes. Where will he live?"

"Right here with me," said the old man. "He's good company for me. He can remember everything."

"I hope he can," said Henry, laughing. "We want to ask him a lot of questions."

"I am afraid we will bother him," said Jessie.

"No bother. He'll like it. I like it too. It's good to see nice young folks like you. I hope you will come often."

"I'm sure we will," said Henry. Then Henry and Jessie walked home.

They found Violet on the back steps reading a big book. She looked up at her brother and sister. They saw at once that she was very much excited.

"Henry!" said Violet. "This is a wonderful book for us! It's all about the Revolutionary War. And it tells how John Hancock and Sam Adams had to hide!"

The two older Aldens sat down beside Violet. "Tell us about it," said Jessie.

"Yes," said Henry. "Go on."

"I found this book in the parlor," said Violet. "See, it has lots of pictures. Here is a picture of that old gun!"

"Just exactly like it!" said Henry, looking at it.

"Now you see," said Violet, "if John Hancock had to hide—"

"There were lots of his men who had to hide, too!" finished Jessie.

"Right!" said Henry. "I know many men were with him, all over the place. You've got something, Violet!"

Benny came around the corner. "What's Violet got?" he asked.

"News," said Henry. "Sit down, Benny. She's found news about our mystery from an old, old book."

He told Benny about it and showed him the pictures.

"This is neat!" cried Benny. "Do you think any of those men hid in our woodshed?"

"Well, no," said Henry slowly. "Not the same woodshed anyway. But a very old one fell down about a hundred years ago. This one is not old enough."

"Goodness!" said Benny. "How old was the old one?"

"It must have been built in Colonial days," said Henry. "What else did you read, Violet?"

"Oh, John Hancock's men got all the guns they could. They got bullets and gunpowder. They hid them in lots of places. One time they hid guns in a load of hay. The Redcoats stood and watched the load of hay go by. They never thought of looking in the hay!"

"Violet!" said Henry. "What a girl you are! This is the best news we have heard."

Benny said, "I wonder what the Redcoats would

have done to the man with the hay cart if they had found the guns?"

"They would have shot him dead!" said Violet.

"Violet!" said Henry again.

"Yes, that's right," said Violet. "There were many brave men in those days. They were always in danger. But they went on getting guns and ammunition and hiding it. The Redcoats were always trying to find it."

"Anything else?" asked Jessie.

"One more thing I read," said Violet. "We lost the battle of Bunker Hill just because we ran out of ammunition."

"Wait a minute," said Henry. "Here comes Sim. Let's ask him something."

They all went to meet Sim. He had a big can of milk for them, and one of cream. Maggie took the cans and Sim looked at the children.

Henry said, "Sim, do you know where the old, *old* woodshed used to be? Not this one, but the one that fell down?"

"Yes, I know that. Right in the very same place."

"Good!" cried Henry. "How do you know?"

Sim scratched his head. "Of course, I wasn't there." He looked at Henry and laughed. "I'm not quite a hundred years old, but my father told me. This woodshed stands right where the old one was. That's all I know."

"That's enough!" cried Jessie. "Do you think anyone hid there from the Redcoats during the war?"

"Maybe. I can't tell you that," said Sim, shaking his head. "Why do you want to know?"

"We just want to find out where all the stories about why nobody will live in this house came from," said Violet softly.

"I see," said Sim. He smiled at Violet. "I'd help you if I could."

"You have," said Benny suddenly. Then as Sim went away he said, "I have an idea!"

"What's your idea?" asked Henry.

"Let's go back to the woodshed and take a flashlight. We might find a clue."

"Not after two hundred years, Benny!" said Jessie.

"I bet nobody ever looked," said Benny. "Of course they didn't find anything if they didn't even look."

After lunch Henry found his big flashlight. Benny found his, too.

"Do come with us, Sam!" begged Violet.

"Go ahead, Sam," said Aunt Jane. "You leave your work whatever it is. This is more important. I don't want to be afraid all my life."

So Sam nodded his head and agreed to go along. He knew that Violet and Benny were safe with Henry and Jessie, but Miss Jane had asked him to go.

Sam had been quietly watching to see if anything unusual were going on around the farm. But not a thing seemed out of place and he had seen no one.

As they came up the hill, Watch walked along with Jessie. But as they came near the woodshed, he put his nose to the ground and ran on ahead. When he reached the door, he ran around the woodshed barking.

Henry kicked the door open. He went in with his flashlight.

"What in the world!" he cried. They all went in. There was the little table back in the corner. There was the bench, the bed, the dishes, the cans, the egg.

The children just stood still and looked at each other.

CHAPTER 8

A Light in the Dark

Benny was the first to speak. He said, "Well, this shows two things. Somebody's living here. And his hiding place can't be very far away."

"That's right, Benny," said Henry. "Nobody could move all these things very far and then move them right back again."

"I say we'd better look for a hole in this cabin," said Benny. "Maybe there's a cellar." He began to flash his light on the floor. Henry did the same. They found nothing.

"This is a funny floor, anyway," said Violet. "Just dirt."

Sam said, "I'd take up that bed and look under it."

"Yes," said Henry. "Sorry, Watch. You'll have to get off the bed."

Benny pushed him off gently. Watch shook himself and sat down.

The children moved the blanket carefully. They moved the thick bed of hay under it.

"Now, look!" said Jessie. "Do you see what I see? That dirt has been moved!"

"That's right, Miss Jessie," said Sam. "And not very long ago either. I wish we had a shovel."

"We don't need a shovel," said Henry. "We need a shingle. And I know exactly where I can find a shingle!"

Henry went over to the shelf and came back with a shingle. "I saw it under the cans the first day," he said. He knelt down and pushed the shingle into the soft dirt. He worked and worked to find a hole or a crack.

"Let me try," said Benny. "I love to dig." He knelt down and began to dig away the dirt.

"Certainly that dirt has been moved," said Violet. "See how soft it is."

Then Benny found the crack.

"I've got it!" he shouted. "It's heavy! I hope I don't break the shingle!"

"Oh, I hope not!" cried Jessie. "Let Henry help you, Benny."

Henry took the shingle and lifted. And up came a cover.

"A wood cover!" shouted Benny. "I bet there's a cellar under this woodshed!"

Perhaps it was not a cellar, but there was surely a big hole under the cover. Some of the dirt fell in. Benny flashed his light down the hole.

"Stairs!" he cried. "I'm going right down!"

His foot was on the top step.

"Oh, no, you're not," said Sam. He shook his head. "I couldn't let you. What would your Aunt Jane say if you got into trouble?"

"What trouble could I get into, Sam? There are only a few stairs."

"Who knows?" said Sam. "Might be somebody down there."

"Oh, no, Sam!" said Benny. "Watch would be right down there by now. And he would bark. And look at him!"

Watch was lying down chewing some hay. He was not interested in the hole.

"I'll go down myself," said Sam. "I'd like to see what's down there."

"You're too tall," said Benny.

"Well, I can bend over," said Sam. "I am going first, that's sure."

"Take the biggest light, Sam," said Henry.

Sam took the big light and put his foot on the first stair. The stair did not break. Sam moved slowly. He sat down on a stair and flashed the light ahead.

The Aldens held their breath.

"Well, what do you know!" he called. "It looks like a tunnel!"

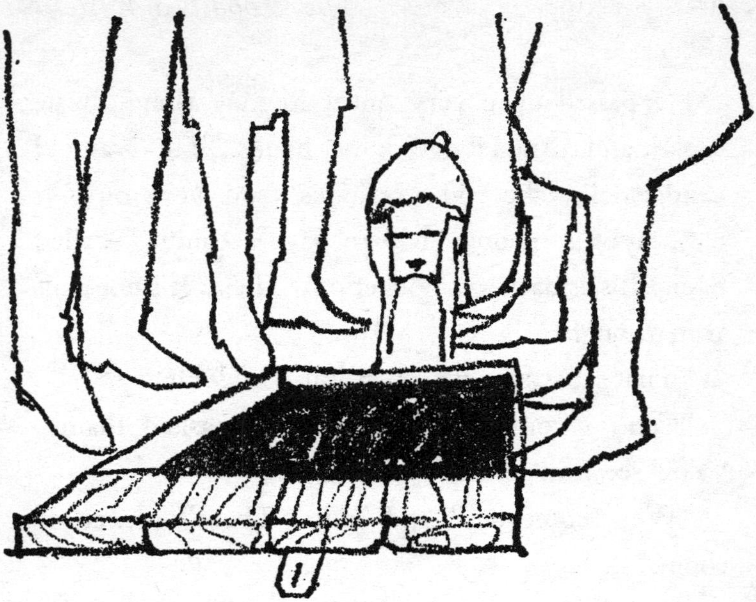

"A tunnel?" called Henry. "Can you crawl through it?"

"Yes, but I'm not going to," said Sam. "Hello, what's this?"

"Well, what is it?" called Henry.

"I don't know. It's something made of tin. I'll bring it up."

He passed up a very queer looking thing. Jessie took it and turned it over in her hands. "This is an old candlestick," she said. "It looks very, very old."

"Maybe somebody had to have a candle," called Sam. "It's as dark as a pocket down here. It's not a bit wet, though."

"That's because it's on a hill," said Henry.

"Can't I come down now, Sam?" asked Benny. "You see how quiet Watch is."

"Well, come on," said Sam. "There's plenty of room."

"Let's *all* go down," cried Benny. But Watch did not like this. He saw Benny go down out of sight. Then when Henry started, he got up and began to bark.

"All right. All right!" said Jessie. "You go down yourself, Mr. Watch." She pushed him gently down the stairs. "You're a bother, though."

"No," said Sam. "Watch is no bother. He's a help."

"Why do you think Watch is a help, Sam?" asked Benny.

"A dog knows," said Sam. "He would bark his head off if there was any danger. A dog can smell danger."

At last everyone had come down the stairs. They had two flashlights.

"It's spooky down here," Jessie said, looking around her and shivering a bit.

"There's your tunnel," said Sam.

Watch ran in, but he soon turned around and came back.

"Maybe it isn't a tunnel, Sam. Maybe it's just a cave," said Henry.

"Maybe," said Sam.

"Here's a lot of junk," said Benny. He kicked a box with his foot. "Ow!" he said. "That box is made of iron!"

"Take it," said Henry. "We can open it later."

"You know what I think?" said Benny. "I think we'd better get out of here. Suppose somebody put that cover on, we'd be in a fix!"

"Right!" said Henry. "We ought to leave somebody up in the cabin to watch out."

Without another word, they all went up the stairs. They put the cover on and stamped on the soft dirt. They put the bed back.

And then they went home to Aunt Jane with a very old candlestick and a very heavy iron box.

CHAPTER 9

What Was in the Box

Aunt Jane was not in the house. No dog came to meet them. Aunt Jane's dog, Lady, always stayed with her. Benny called out, "Aunt Jane!" When nobody answered, Henry called, "Lady! Lady!"

A bark came from the yard behind the house. There sat Aunt Jane reading Violet's big book. She looked up.

"Well, how did you get along?" she asked.

Benny could hardly wait to tell her about the hole under the woodshed. Then Jessie gave her the old candlestick.

"What an old candlestick!" cried Aunt Jane. "This is the kind they used at the time of the Revolutionary War!"

"That's what Jessie thought, Aunt Jane," said Violet. "And we found an old iron box, too."

"Open it right away!" said Aunt Jane. "It looks like a candle box. The kind they used to pack candles in."

"Somebody sat there in the dark with a candle," said Henry. "Why would they do that, Aunt Jane?"

"I have an idea, Henry! I got it from this old book. You just open that box and we'll see."

"I'll have to break the top off, I'm afraid," said Henry. "See how rusty it is."

"All right. Break it!" cried Aunt Jane.

"I'll get a hammer and chisel," shouted Benny. "I'll be right back."

Off he went to the house. He soon came back and

Henry started to work. Little by little the cover opened. At last it fell off.

"Well, what is it?" cried Benny. "Just a lot of old black powder."

"Gunpowder!" said Aunt Jane with shining eyes. "I read about gunpowder in Violet's book. Somebody dug that hole to keep ammunition in!"

"You're right," said Henry quietly. "I think we have found one of the places where they hid ammunition!"

"Then they took it to Concord," said Jessie.

"In a load of hay!" said Violet.

They all looked at each other.

Henry said, "Aunt Jane, we decided not to go into the tunnel. We may find a lot more things later."

"We thought somebody might shut the cover down," said Benny. "And there we'd all be. Next time we'll leave somebody outside to keep watch. Where's Sam?"

But Sam had gone back to work.

Aunt Jane said, "Sam must go with you every time. Remember that."

"I think so, too," said Jessie. "That dirt looked as if it had been moved only yesterday. Some stranger is around here."

"He's stealing eggs from the Beans," said Benny. Everyone laughed.

Benny went on slowly. Talking about the Beans

had made him think of something. He said, "Aunt Jane, why didn't you marry this Andy Bean?"

"All right, I'll tell you, Benny. Nobody ever asked me before."

"I wasn't very polite to ask you, was I?" said Benny.

"No," said Aunt Jane. "But I don't mind. I was quite silly. Andy Bean did ask me to marry him and I said no. My reasons were very silly. I know that now. The first reason was that he was two years younger than I was, but he was big and he looked older. What do you guess the second reason was?"

"What?" asked four voices.

"I didn't want to be called Mrs. Bean!"

Violet patted Aunt Jane's hand. "I don't think that was too silly."

"Well, I do," said Aunt Jane. "I have been sorry a thousand times. Andy was a fine looking, clever boy. He had a nice crooked smile. His younger brother owns the Bean farm now. His wife is the Mrs. Bean who told you about the eggs, Benny."

"Don't we have the most exciting adventures!" cried Benny. "Something new is always happening."

"Yes, Benny," said Aunt Jane laughing. "Ever since I met you something nice has happened every day. Before that nothing happened."

"Well, tomorrow we'll explore that cellar again," said Henry. "I'll read that old book myself. I'd like to know what to look for."

"We might find an old gun," said Benny. "Maybe an old flintlock."

"Benny Alden!" cried Violet. Her eyes were like stars. "Do you know what you just said? Maybe that cellar is where Andy Bean found his old flintlock!"

Everyone was excited until Jessie said, "No, I don't think so. Don't you remember that somebody gave it to Andy?"

"That's right, Jessie," said Benny. "They said it was somebody hiding in this house! And that's why the stories have been told and nobody will live here."

"Well!" said Henry. "We'll find out if it takes all summer."

"Don't forget," said Aunt Jane softly, "it *may*."

Henry smiled at his aunt. Maybe it would take all summer, but the mystery would be solved. And it would be solved quickly if some of his and Benny's ideas proved to be right.

CHAPTER 10

Back to the Woodshed

The next day Maggie saw an old man in overalls coming to the back door. He had a basket of eggs.

"Are you selling eggs?" Maggie asked.

"Yep," said the old man.

"Where did you come from?" she asked again.

"Beans'," said the man.

Benny heard him from the next room. He laughed. He said to Violet, "He doesn't talk much, does he?"

"I wonder who he is?" said Violet.

"I know who he is," said Benny. "He is the Beans' hired man. I saw him working there when I went over."

Maggie told the man, "We will have plenty of eggs later. Sam is going to raise chickens."

"Yep," said the man.

"We do want two dozen eggs now," Maggie went on. "Put them in this pan."

Benny and Violet listened.

"Have you lost any more eggs?" asked Maggie.

"Yep," said the man.

"Can't you say anything but 'yep'?" Maggie laughed.

"No," said the man. He did not laugh.

"Well, come every week," said Maggie. "What's your name?"

"Willie," said the man.

"My, my! A grown man called Willie! You ought to be William."

The man did not answer. Then he left.

Benny went into the kitchen at once. "What's the

matter with him?" he asked. "Can't he talk?"

"Well," said Maggie, "he doesn't act very smart to me. Maybe he doesn't know very much. Not very bright. He can't help that. Maybe he's a good worker. He sells very nice eggs."

"Hi! Come on!" called Henry from outside. "I've got a bigger flashlight this time. It will last longer."

Very soon Henry, Benny, and the two girls were on their way to the woodshed. Sam had to stop his work and go with them.

"I'll never get anything done," said Sam. But he smiled.

"I don't think it will be much longer now," said Henry mysteriously. "Do any of you know why all those things were taken out of the woodshed?"

"I think I do," said Violet. "Somebody found my flowers on the table."

"Right!" said Henry. "And then why were the things put back?"

"I bet someone saw us," said Benny, "and said, 'Oh, it's only children!' "

"Good, Benny. That's what I think too," replied Henry. "We'll be careful this time to leave everything just as it is now."

"Do you want me to stay outside and watch?" asked Sam.

"Yes, I think that would be best, wouldn't it?" said Jessie. "We'll take Watch down in the hole with us. If you see anyone, just call."

Soon the four children and the dog were down in the hole. The flashlight was very bright.

"Almost as bright as day," said Benny, looking around. Watch was already in the tunnel, smelling around, wagging his tail. Henry followed him. He had to bend over.

Soon Henry called back, "This isn't a tunnel! It's just a big room. I can almost stand up."

Jessie followed him. She said, "This was certainly a storehouse. All kinds of things are on the floor. Don't fall over them."

Benny came in. He said, "Let's put the light in the middle, Henry. Then we can look at every single thing. What are the little red balls all over the floor?"

"I think they are bullets," said Henry. "They are all rusty. That makes them look red. Pick them all up."

"Oh, Violet, I wish we had a bag!" cried Jessie.

"We have," said Violet. She held up what looked like a small, folded piece of cloth. But when she shook it out, it was a large bag folded up many times. When it was open, it was enormous.

"How do you think of everything, Violet?" said Jessie. "That will hold all we find."

"All but this," shouted Benny. He dug out a flintlock. It was almost buried in the dirt.

"Just exactly like the other!" cried Violet.

"That settles it," said Henry. "This was a hiding place for ammunition."

Jessie added, "Only somebody has been here lately. It must be the one who lives in this woodshed."

"I just wonder who it could be!" said Violet. "Who would want to hide here these days?"

"Look here!" cried Jessie. "I almost fell over this!" She held up an old milking stool with three legs.

Henry looked at it. "I can just see one of those soldiers sitting on that stool with a candle!"

"What do you see him doing, Henry?" asked Benny.

"Well, packing bullets and cartridges and gunpowder in candle boxes."

At last they could not find anything more. They went up the steps and put the cover over the hole. Then they went home with their treasures. Sam had not seen anyone.

When Aunt Jane had seen everything, she looked at the four children. She said, "I think we are soon going to find a very exciting story. Mr. Cole has come to spend the summer with his brother, and he wants to see you right away!"

CHAPTER 11

A New Discovery

Henry said, "We certainly want to see Mr. Cole right away. I hope he has something to tell us."

"I hope he will talk more than Willie," said Benny.

They all laughed as they started out for Grandpa Cole's.

The two old men were sitting side by side in two chairs in the yard.

"They look a lot alike, don't they?" said Jessie. "But we know they are not twins. How exciting this is! We may get news and we may not."

"Be prepared," said Benny. "Just like the Boy Scouts."

The two Mr. Coles were delighted to see the visitors. "Go and get four chairs," said Grandpa.

"Oh, no, we can sit on the grass," said Jessie. "We like it." They all sat down, so it was too late to get chairs.

"We are very glad you came at last, sir," said Henry to Mr. Cole. "We have been waiting for you. Maybe you can tell us something new."

"Well, my boy, I think I can," said Mr. Cole. "I knew Andy Bean very well. I was a young man and Andy was just a big boy. Always up to something. He was good looking with a one-sided kind of smile. He always wanted to do exciting things. And we were quiet people."

"We always come right back to Andy Bean, don't we?" said Benny.

"Yes, your mystery is about Andy Bean, that's why. I'm sure of that. You see I knew he had that flintlock."

"You did!" they all said.

"Yes. He came and showed it to me as a secret. But I didn't think much about it because I didn't know how to shoot it."

"Didn't Andy know?" asked Violet.

"No. That's why he took it up into the woods to fool with it. He had gunpowder and matches. But I suppose the gun was too rusty. So before he knew it, he had started a big fire. The leaves and grass were very dry and caught fire easily. The farmhouse was saved, but many trees were burned. I suppose Andy was afraid somebody would put him in jail. He never could stand being shut in, so he ran away."

"He left the gun," said Henry.

"Yes, he left the gun. But this isn't what I wanted to tell you. You knew this already, didn't you?"

"Most of it," said Henry. "But we hope you know things we don't. People keep saying someone at our house hid there and gave Andy the flintlock."

"Not a bit of truth to it," Mr. Cole said loudly. "People like to tell tales just to scare themselves. Andy told me he found the gun somewhere in your house. He didn't say where. But he did say, 'I found the whole story, too, all written out.' Those were his own words. Then he said, 'The other end is in the woodshed.' "

"I wonder what he meant? The other end of what?" cried Violet.

"I never knew," said Mr. Cole sadly. "Now I'm sorry I didn't ask him, but then I didn't think it was important."

"Is there anyone else we could ask?" said Jessie. "Who else was around here at that time?"

"Oh, Willie," said Mr. Cole laughing. "But you won't get much out of Willie!"

"No, he doesn't talk," said Benny.

"No, he doesn't talk, and he doesn't know much either. He was born that way. He can't help it. But he was around here then, sure enough."

Violet said, "Do you think there could be a tunnel between the woodshed and our house?"

"No, it's too far. But if I were you, I'd hunt around in your own cellar. For Andy said the woodshed is the other end of *something*."

"We'll do that right off," said Henry getting up. "Do you think we might find this mystery written down?"

"It looks that way to me," said Mr. Cole. "Something happened in your house. That's what makes the mystery. People had always felt there was something unusual about the old place. After Andy Bean's disappearance, there were more stories whispered around."

"That's what makes it so exciting," said Benny.

"You are new," said Grandpa Cole. "You never lived here long ago with all these goings-on."

"Thanks a million," said Henry. "You helped us a lot, Mr. Cole. We'll tell you what we find."

The Aldens could hardly wait to get to their own cellar. Violet stopped to tell Aunt Jane all about it.

Then she went down the cellar with the rest.

Henry was standing still, looking all around. He laughed and said, "Benny, where would you begin? You have good luck finding things."

Benny was very much pleased. He said at once, "The potato pit. You can see everything else. But you can't see the inside of the potato pit."

"OK," said Henry. "You and I will be the ones to get dirty. In you go!" He helped his little brother over the edge of the empty pit. He handed down a flashlight and a small shovel. Then he took an axe and jumped in.

Jessie and Violet could see the top of his head.

"How are you going to get out?" asked Jessie as she looked down.

"You can give us a box to step on," said Henry. "But we haven't begun yet."

First the boys looked at the floor very carefully. They found nothing but dirt. Then they began to look at the walls.

"These walls are made of stones, aren't they,

Henry?" asked Benny. "And then plaster over them?"

"Right," said Henry. "But maybe some of them are loose."

He hit the wall with his axehead and said, "Listen! This isn't stone. It's wood!"

"Don't tell me!" shouted Benny. "Maybe it's a little wooden door! And all covered with plaster!"

The boys pounded away at the door. The plaster fell off in big pieces. At last they could open the door. What a noise it made as it opened!

The boys flashed the light in the door. "A big hole!" cried Benny. "Just exactly like the hole under the woodshed! This is the other end of something, whatever it is!"

CHAPTER 12

Too Much Excitement

"Oh, tell us what you see!" begged Jessie. "Can't we come down, too?"

"I wouldn't, Jessie," said Henry looking up. "It's so dirty. We'll look very carefully and tell you everything."

Benny had crawled through the little door with the light. "The very same things!" he shouted. "A milking stool and an old candlestick and some more iron boxes! We'll bring them all up."

"How big is the hole?" called Violet.

"Just big enough for two people to sit down. You can't stand up," Benny called back. "Oh, boy! Here is an old plate! And here's an old cup! All broken!"

His voice sounded strange and far away, but they could tell how excited Benny was.

"Hand them to me, old fellow," said Henry. "And you let me have a turn in there."

Benny crawled out and Henry crawled in.

"Find anything, Henry?" called Jessie.

"Well, yes! This seems to be a spoon. An awfully old spoon. Somebody ate in here all right."

But that was all. Henry handed the things up to the girls. Jessie gave him a box to step on and the boys jumped out of the hole.

Henry took some things and started for the kitchen. There was Sam, sitting on the cellar stairs.

"Well, Sam," said Henry. "How long have you been here?"

"Ever since you came down," said Sam. "Your aunt told me to."

"But we weren't in any danger in our own cellar," said Henry. "Sometimes Aunt Jane treats us like little children."

Sam grinned a bit and said, "To tell the truth, I guess I want to know what's going on. I'll help you carry that stuff outdoors."

Soon everything was spread out on the grass in front of Aunt Jane.

The boxes held gunpowder and bullets. There were no guns this time. Aunt Jane looked at everything. She said, "Now, we know a little bit more.

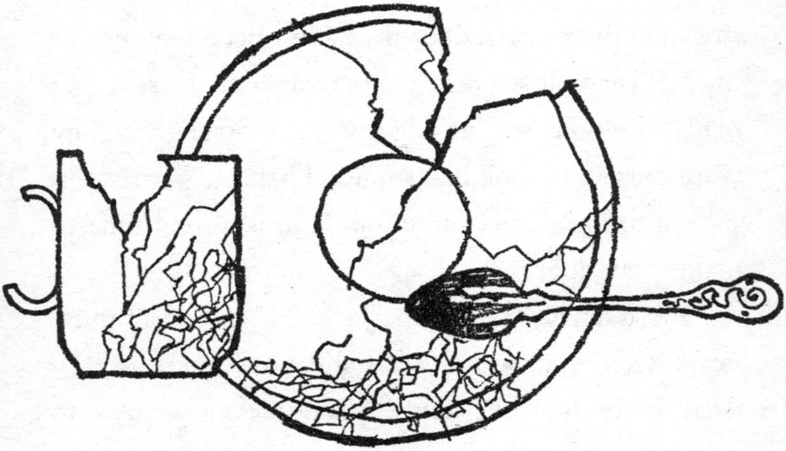

This plate is over two hundred years old. And we know there were two hiding places."

"Why should people want to hide?" asked Benny. "They just wanted to hide their ammunition."

"Yes, Benny," Violet said. "But you see the Redcoats wanted to catch the men, too. I'm sure someone hid in both these caves. Someone sat on that milking stool and ate from that plate."

"Good for you, Violet," said Henry, smiling. "I'm sure you are right."

Then he said to Aunt Jane, "Let me tell you about that door in the potato pit. I would never have dreamed there was a door if I hadn't been looking for one. A very clever man made that door. First it was made of wood, but the edges were not straight. They were curved to look like stones. Then the plaster was put on to look like stones, too. It took a long time to make that door."

"Yes, Henry," said Aunt Jane. "Think of all those years when your grandfather and I lived here as children. Nobody ever found that door. And we used to play hide and seek in that hole. We poured potatoes into it and hid in the potatoes."

"I wonder if Grandfather would have any ideas," said Jessie slowly. "I know he had to go back to work. But he might remember something."

Everyone looked thoughtful for a moment.

"Oh, I'm all tired out thinking!" cried Aunt Jane suddenly. "It must be suppertime." She looked tired and almost as if she were going to cry.

"Dear Aunt Jane!" cried Violet. "This is too exciting for you. I'll tell Maggie to get supper right away. I'll help her."

"So will I," said Jessie quietly. "We'll get supper in two shakes."

The three worked as fast as they could to get supper on the table. In no time, Maggie went to get Aunt Jane.

"We have your favorite things, Miss Jane," she said. "Chicken salad and hot rolls and early asparagus."

"And a cup of good strong tea, I hope," said Aunt Jane.

"Yes, sure enough, a cup of good strong tea," said Maggie. She helped Aunt Jane into her chair at the table. Maggie was a bit worried. She said so to Jessie when they were getting supper. "Your Aunt Jane must be getting too tired. She doesn't ever speak quickly like that any more."

"We'll be more careful of her," said Jessie. "We mustn't upset Aunt Jane."

"Maybe all this talk is too much for her," said Violet. "You must remember that once upon a time she really loved Andy Bean."

"I suppose she did," said Maggie. "But that was a long time ago."

"But this brings it back," said Violet quietly.

Aunt Jane ate her supper well and drank her tea. As the family finished eating, they heard a voice talking to Maggie in the kitchen.

"It's only Willie," Henry said. "He must be selling Maggie some more asparagus."

"Good," said Benny. "I hope she will buy it."

Benny had not heard the talk about Aunt Jane. He

went on now with his own ideas. "But to go back to Andy Bean. Mr. Cole said there was a written story somewhere. Where do you suppose that story ever went? And what did it say? And where did Andy get it?"

Suddenly Aunt Jane's cheeks looked bright pink. She spoke quickly and, for her, quite loudly. It was hard for the children to tell whether she was angry or just tired.

"Andy Bean!" she exclaimed. "All the trouble he's made! Running away and all. I'd like to shoot Andy Bean!"

Everyone turned in surprise toward Aunt Jane. She had not sounded like this for a long, long time.

Henry was by her side in a second. "Don't you worry any more, Aunt Jane!" he said in a loving voice. "Come on, I'll carry you to bed!"

"No, Henry! Really, I'm all right."

But Jessie and Violet and Maggie rushed over to her. Henry lifted his tiny aunt very easily and carried her to bed. By that time she was laughing.

"I'm so sorry," she said. "I just got to thinking how nice it would have been if Andy hadn't run away!"

"It's all right, Miss Jane," said Maggie. "Put on your very best lacy nightdress and you'll go to sleep early."

Maggie sat by Aunt Jane until she fell asleep.

Benny and Henry bought the asparagus and paid Willie.

"Did you work for Andy Bean's father?" asked Benny.

"Yep."

"Don't bother Willie. He couldn't have been more than a boy then," Henry said to his brother. "Just put the asparagus in the refrigerator. Then we'll go outdoors and talk all we want. I hope tomorrow Aunt Jane will be herself again."

CHAPTER 13

Just in Time!

Aunt Jane was all right the next day. But she was surprised when Henry said he wanted to go up to the woodshed again.

"Why?" she asked.

"Well," said Henry, "if someone lives there, we might find something new any day."

"Take Sam with you," said Aunt Jane as usual.

"Poor Sam!" said Benny. "He doesn't want to go."

"Well, I don't know," said Sam. "I'm getting interested in this woodshed."

They could not find Watch so they went along without him.

Soon the five of them reached the woodshed. Everything was in order. There was one egg on the shelf. As they stood there, they heard somebody coming through the woods.

"Quick!" whispered Henry. "Someone's coming. Climb that tree!"

A tall tree stood right by the door. Even Violet was good at climbing trees. She went first. Benny was after her in a flash. "Hurry!" he whispered to Jessie. He went out of sight in the heavy leaves. He gave Jessie his hand and helped her up. Henry was last.

"Not me," said Sam. "I'll wait and see who it is."

Henry looked down and then whispered to Jessie, "It's *Willie!* I wonder what he wants."

Sam stood still. When Willie came out of the bushes Sam said, "Hello, Willie."

"Hello," said Willie. He just stood there.

"What are you going to do, Willie?" asked Sam.

"Take the things," said Willie.

"What things?"

Willie pointed at the dishes and the table. He did not speak.

"Are the dishes yours?" asked Sam.

"No." Willie shook his head.

Sam said kindly, "Who do they belong to, Willie?"

"Andy Bean," said Willie. He said it as if Andy had always lived at home.

"Andy *Bean?* Is Andy around here now?"

"No, not now. Went on the bus."

"Has Andy Bean been living here in this woodshed?"

"Yep," said Willie.

"Why in the world did he go away on a bus?" Sam asked.

"Going away to sea," said Willie.

"But *why?*" asked Sam again.

"She hates him. She'd shoot him," said Willie, nodding his head.

"Shoot him? Miss Jane wouldn't shoot him!"

They all stared in surprise at Willie.

"Yep," said Willie. "She said so. I heard her. 'I'd like to shoot Andy Bean,' she said."

Henry looked up at Jessie and without a word he slid down the tree. All the rest came after him.

"What? What?" cried Willie when he saw the children come out of the tree.

"Come on, Sam!" shouted Henry. "We must catch Andy!"

"No," said Willie. His mouth was open. "He took the bus."

But the Aldens and Sam were running down the hill. Benny shouted back, "Aunt Jane doesn't hate him, Willie! She was just fooling!"

"Don't stop to talk," cried Jessie. "We must catch that bus!"

"We can't," Sam called back. "It's been gone fifteen minutes."

"Well, we've *got* to catch it," cried Benny. "It has to stop to let people off!"

They ran to Sam's old car which stood in the yard. They all threw themselves into the car and off they went. Benny and Henry sat beside Sam. For a minute they could not speak. When Henry got his breath, he said, "I bet Andy came home and found out Aunt Jane was back. He must have wondered if she would see him."

Benny said, "I bet so, too. And I remember what Aunt Jane said. She said, 'I'd like to shoot Andy Bean!' "

Jessie added, "And Willie was right in the kitchen selling asparagus. He heard every word!"

"Oh, dear, how wrong can you be?" said Violet. "Willie didn't know Aunt Jane didn't mean it. So he told Andy, and Andy went away again."

"Drive faster if you can, Sam," said Henry. "If Andy gets out at the bus station he will get on the train. Then we'll be too late to stop him."

Jessie said, "We don't even know that he took this bus."

"Yes," said Sam. "This is the only bus in the morning. He'd have to take it. But what shall we do when we catch up with the bus?"

"Well, we know he has a crooked smile," said Henry. "We can tell him he is wrong about Aunt Jane. Let Violet tell him. He'll believe *her*." He smiled at Violet.

"But how do we stop the bus driver? That's the question," said Jessie.

Benny said, "That's easy. If we see the bus, you honk your horn, Sam, and we can shout to the driver."

"This old car is surprised it can go so fast," said Sam. "And I am, too."

The old car rattled and squeaked. But it flew along.

At last Benny cried, "There's the blue bus! Oh, Sam, honk your horn!"

Sam kept the horn going. The bus driver honked back. He looked in his mirror at the children. Then he pointed at the railroad station ahead. There stood the train, ready to go.

When the bus stopped, the driver put his head out of the window and said, "What's the matter with you? Want to get on?"

"No," said Henry. "We'll tell you in a minute." They all piled out of the car and ran around to the door of the bus.

Benny cried, "Have you got a big man on board? He has a crooked smile!"

"Well, I don't know about the smile," said the driver laughing. "But I have a man on board on the back seat. Just coming out."

They looked back in the bus and saw a tall man coming out. His hair was brown, not white.

"Oh, excuse me!" cried Benny. "Are you Andy Bean?"

"Yes, that's my name," said the stranger. "Why?" He stared at Violet. Then he smiled. His smile was crooked. He came a few steps toward the Aldens.

"Oh, please," said Violet. "Aunt Jane sent us to find you! Don't run away again until we tell you all about it."

"Aunt *Jane!*" exclaimed the man. He shook his head and turned toward the train. "No, Jane doesn't want to see me," he said. "And that's that."

"Please come and sit in our car," begged Violet. "Aunt Jane wants very much to see you."

"She said she hated me and maybe she has a reason to. She talked about shooting," Andy Bean said in a low voice.

"Oh, you don't understand," said Henry. "That was what Willie said, wasn't it? Aunt Jane didn't mean it. She just got too tired and spoke that way. She must have been like that even when she was a girl."

"I wish I could believe you," said Andy.

Now Sam spoke. "You can. You can believe anything these kids say. They know what they're doing every time."

Andy looked at Sam. Then he looked at the children. "All right," he said. "I'll give it one more try. I'll go back with you if that's what you want."

"Yes, indeed!" said Jessie. That's exactly what we want."

Andy had a small bag, and Henry said, "I'll put your bag in the trunk."

"No, thank you," said Andy Bean with his crooked smile, "I always keep this bag with me wherever I go."

It was not a large bag. Benny at once began to guess what might be in it. A change of clothes? A treasure map? Pistols? His guessing turned into a game, but he had to wait for the answer.

CHAPTER 14

A Treasure Bag

Sam drove home slowly. Violet and Benny sat on the front seat. This made room for Andy on the back seat with Henry and Jessie.

"Now the next thing is to tell Aunt Jane," said Jessie. "I am worried about that."

"Oh, that will be easy," said Andy Bean. "I'll tell her myself."

"What will you tell her?" Violet asked softly.

"Well, I came home to Boston on a ship. I saw in the paper that the Aldens had bought the old house.

So I thought I'd come up and see if I was welcome. I knew Willie would keep my secret. He knew me right away."

"You were the one stealing all those eggs!" said Benny.

Andy laughed. "Well, they were really my own eggs, you see. Half that Bean farm belongs to me."

"What will your brother say?" asked Henry. "You have been away so long."

"I don't want the farm," Andy said. "Don't you worry about me. The only thing is Jane. If she wants me to stay, that's all I care about."

They soon drove up to their own back door. "Oh, dear!" said Violet, "This is going to be so hard for Aunt Jane. She thinks you may be dead. She isn't very strong."

"That's one reason I came home," said Andy. "I'm strong enough for two."

And he looked it.

Aunt Jane was sitting in her long chair in the back yard. She was shelling peas. She looked up at the children. Then she saw the stranger smiling at her. Her face changed. She cried, "Andy! Andy! You did come back! Henry, get a chair!"

"I don't need a chair, Jane," said Andy. He went over to the little lady and took her hand. "Glad to see me, Jane?"

"Oh, yes! I'd know you anywhere. Will you stay?"

"You bet I'll stay!" said the tall man. "I have a long story to tell. But first I have something for you. Everywhere I went, I bought one of these for you."

He took the pan of shelled peas out of her lap and gave her a small bag. "Open it."

The children sat down on the grass. Andy sat down beside Aunt Jane. He did not seem old at all. Aunt Jane opened the bag and took out a box. She opened the box and looked in.

"They look like old, old stones," said Benny.

"Very good, young feller," said Andy. "That's just what they are. Old, old stones." He laughed.

Aunt Jane picked one up and looked at it carefully. It was not round. It was not square. It was very different looking. But Jessie saw a flash as the stone turned. "It's blue!" she said.

"Yes, that one is blue," said Andy. "It's a sapphire. These stones are not cut. Just as they came from the ground. I got that one in India. Everywhere I went, I bought you a jewel, Jane. Look at this one!" He picked up a stone that flashed green.

"An emerald!" said Aunt Jane. "It is enormous! These must have cost you a fortune, Andrew."

"Well, I didn't want a fortune," said Andy. "I wanted adventure. But now I'm through with adventure."

"I don't believe a word of it!" cried Aunt Jane, but she looked at Andy proudly.

Benny said, "Why didn't you come home long ago?"

Andy said with a crooked smile, "You wouldn't believe me if I told you."

"Yes, I would," said Benny nodding his head.

"I was afraid of Jane," said Andy, speaking quietly. "She's a tiny little thing, but I was afraid of her. And she left, too, to go out West. What was there to come back for?"

Jessie said, "I can understand. If Aunt Jane turned you down, you'd have nothing to live for."

"That is exactly right, young lady," cried Andy. "You have a lot of good sense."

Aunt Jane looked at the jewels one by one. "For me?" she said. "I don't need them all. Andy, let's

have the children each choose one to keep. I want them each to have a jewel."

"Oh, boy!" said Benny. "I can tell you what everyone will choose."

"All right. Go ahead, boy," said Andy.

"Jessie will take a blue sapphire, Violet will take a purple amethyst, Henry will take a green emerald, and I will take a red ruby."

"Right!" shouted everyone.

"There is a fortune in that box, sure enough," said Andy. "But I found something under the woodshed that I think is more exciting."

"Always looking for excitement, Andy," said Aunt Jane smiling.

"Yes, I suppose I always will be," said Andy. "But I am glad to stay at home now. I shall find plenty of excitement right here."

"When are you going to show us what you found in the woodshed?" asked Benny.

"Oh, let's wait!" Jessie said, looking at Aunt Jane and Andy Bean. "I'm sure that everyone is hungry."

"Thank you," said Andy. "I am hungry. What I found can wait a little longer."

"Mercy!" cried Aunt Jane. "Andy's hungry! Benny, run and tell Maggie to have lunch just as soon as she can."

"No eggs!" Andrew called after him. "I'm sick of eggs."

"I'll tell Maggie," shouted Benny. "But I'm sure lunch isn't all eggs anyway!"

CHAPTER 15

Letter from Long Ago

Maggie did not have eggs for lunch. She had a good meal for a strong man. She had cold meat and a hot dish of macaroni and cheese. Andy ate as if he were half starved.

"I've had cold food for a long time," he said. "Even raw eggs."

"We'll soon fix that," said Aunt Jane. She loved to see him eat.

Benny said, "Right after lunch are you going to show us that thing you found?"

"Right! Just as soon as lunch is over. I have it right here in my pocket. Maybe you won't think much of it. But I do."

"I'm sure we will," said Jessie, "if you found it in the woodshed. That's an exciting place."

"Yes, and so is your own cellar," said Andrew.

At last he could not eat any more. He said, "All right. Come out in the yard again and see my treasure. This is in a bag too."

When Aunt Jane was in her chair, Andy gave her a leather bag.

"What a funny looking bag!" said Benny. "It must be very old."

Aunt Jane opened the bag. It was stained and ready to fall apart. Inside was another piece of leather. Inside that was an old paper covered with writing.

"The ink is brown," said Violet.

Aunt Jane carefully unfolded the paper. "It is dated June, 1775," she said. "Shall I read it?"

"Yes," said Benny. "Just as quick as you can."

Now at last the whole story would be told.

So Aunt Jane began to read. She read slowly because sometimes the writing was hard to read.

My name is Mary Cooper and my husband is called James. I am telling my true story just as it happened. When the war is over, I hope someone will find it. Then they will know why we did what we did. My husband and I love this country and we want it to be free. But we are in great danger. We are storing ammunition on our farm. A man who loves liberty came and asked my husband if we would do this, and he said yes.

Where could we hide it? We thought of two places. One was in a woodshed on the hill. The other was in our cellar in the potato pit.

One night James said to me, "Mary, the men who come here with ammunition are in danger. Perhaps we could hide them somewhere."

"In the same place with the guns and bullets," I said.

So we began to dig under the woodshed to make a place to hide the men. We had to work at night. I went with James and helped him dig. It was very hard, but at last we had a big hole. We put in a stool and a candle. Then we dug another hole in the potato pit. This was harder. James made a door to look like the stones. But it was very good. I could hardly see it myself.

One night there was a great knocking on our door. We got up and went to the door. There stood a Redcoat holding a poor man by the arms.

The Redcoat said, "I caught this man hiding ammunition. We want to know if there were others with him."

James said, "I have not seen anyone."

I said, "Bring the poor man into the kitchen. He looks half dead."

The man laughed. "Soon he will be dead. I am taking him to Boston. He will be hanged as he deserves."

"I have a plan," said my husband. "Let us talk it over. You will want a horse and food. Put this man down in my cellar. There is no door to the outside, so he cannot run away."

"How can I believe you?" asked the soldier.

"Here," said James, "take these two chairs. You and I will sit at the head of the cellar stairs by this door. We will know if he comes up."

When the poor man was thrown down the cellar stairs, James whispered to him "*Potato pit.*" How I hoped he would understand! We had planned to dig a tunnel from the cellar to the woodshed, but it was too hard.

James had to give a horse to the Redcoat. He would have been shot if he had not. I went out to the barn and got the horse out. We owned four horses. Then the Redcoat went to the cellar stairs and called, "Come up, you!" But nobody came. We all went down the cellar. The Redcoat hunted and hunted. He said to James, "You have let him escape."

James said truly, "You sat right here yourself all the time. There is no other door to the outside."

The Redcoat was angry. He could not find the poor man. So he rode away. He said he would come back, but he never did.

When he had gone, we took the poor man upstairs to the kitchen and gave him food. Then we told him to hide in the hole under the woodshed until we came for him. That night we went up and got him. We gave him a horse and the ammunition and he rode away and we never saw him again, either.

We hid many men in those two places. I am so unhappy that we could not be friendly with our neighbors. But we were afraid someone would tell what we were doing. We never let anyone come to see us and we never went to see anyone, so we lost all the friends we had. In those days we could not tell who was a friend and who was an enemy. I hope we did our share to make this country free, but in doing so, we lost all our friends.

MARY COOPER

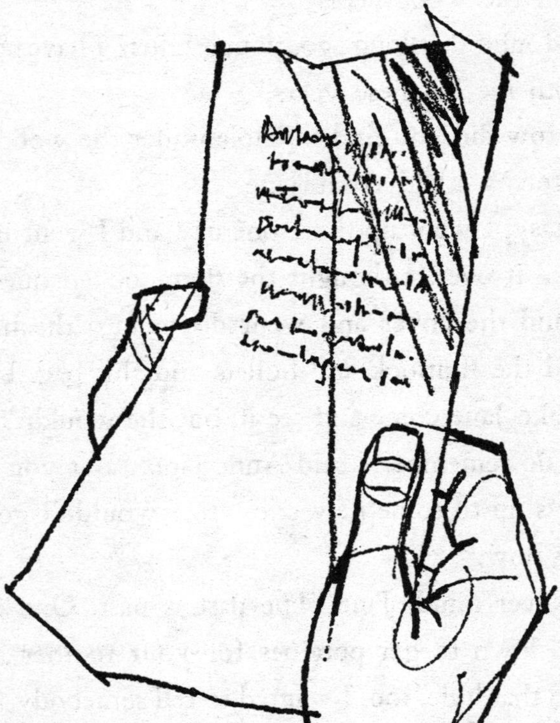

Of course Benny was the first to speak. He said, "Isn't that too bad? To lose all their friends? But they helped win the war, that's sure. Did you find this in the woodshed?"

"I found that long ago, young feller! I have carried it with me all these years."

"How did you find the hole under the woodshed, Andrew?" asked Aunt Jane.

"Easy, I went up there one day and I went in and looked it over. I thought the floor looked queer, so I found the cover and went down into the hole. I found the flintlock and bullets and this bag. I tried to make Jane come and see it, but she wouldn't go."

"I do remember," said Aunt Jane. "But you were always up to some new trick, so I wouldn't go. I'm sorry now."

"Never mind, Jane. The past is past. One day I went down to get potatoes for your mother and I found that hole, too. I wanted to tell somebody, but I didn't dare. At last I showed the gun to John Cole, but he wasn't interested. He said he didn't know how to shoot it. He wasn't interested in the story, either. So I didn't even read it to him."

Henry looked thoughtful. "I think I see now," he said. "Way back, Mary Cooper acted so queerly that at last no one had anything to do with her. I suppose people began to make up stories to explain why they wouldn't go to the Cooper place. Finally I expect that no one remembered how it all started. People just knew there was something mysterious about the farm. And if anything new went wrong, someone was always ready to say, 'Well, what can you expect?' "

Andrew looked at Henry and nodded. "I think you understand the people around here. Sometimes they act just that way."

"All those ideas about something wrong with this place lasted a long, long time," said Jessie. "We'll have to tell the real story now."

"Don't worry!" cried Andrew. "When people see me, the story will go like wild fire. It may even be in the Sunday papers!"

Aunt Jane was laughing. "You'll put it in the Sunday papers yourself! My, my! It will be exciting living with you, Andy!"

"What?" cried Andy. "Did you say living with me, Jane? You kids just run off and let me talk to your aunt!"

In one minute the young Aldens were on the other side of the house. They sat down on the back step. Maggie came to the door. "Is Miss Jane all right?" she asked.

"She's fine," said Benny. "I think she's going to marry Andy Bean. Then she'll be Mrs. Bean after all."

"I hope so," said Maggie.

"Do you?" asked Jessie.

"Yes, I do. I feel homesick for the West. Sam and his wife feel the same way. If Miss Jane was in good hands, we'd all go back to the ranch country."

Henry said, "Andy won't be a very good farmer, but he's a strong man and Aunt Jane can hire men to run the farm."

"I just wonder what Andy will find for excitement up here?" said Jessie.

"Maybe he'll take Aunt Jane on trips," said Benny.

"Oh, but she isn't strong enough to go on trips!" cried Violet.

Maggie said, "My dear girl, your Aunt Jane is strong enough to do anything she *wants* to do. And if she doesn't want to, she's as weak as a rag."

"That's right," said Benny. "I'm even like that myself."

CHAPTER 16

Aunt Jane's Surprise

At supper, Aunt Jane said to everyone, "I have something special to tell all of you."

She stopped and smiled at Andrew Bean, then went on, "Andy and I are no longer young, but we are going to be married. We are not going to wait any longer!"

Jessie and Violet jumped up and kissed their aunt. Henry took her hand, but Benny just smiled from ear to ear.

Then everyone turned toward Andy and soon it seemed as if the most wonderful kind of party had begun.

"From now on," Andy said, "Jane and I will share our adventures. I promise you that."

Benny said, "Do you want to run the farm, Uncle Andy?"

"Don't call me uncle! You started with Andy. Keep on with Andy. No, I'm not a very good farmer. But I can get plenty of help to run the farm."

"How about Willie?" asked Benny. "He's a good farmer."

"Right," said Andy. "He can handle growing things."

"He doesn't talk much, does he?" said Benny.

"No, he's not a talker," agreed Andy.

"We didn't guess for a long time he knew part of the mystery," said Henry.

By now the whole meal was over, and the whole family moved outdoors to sit together in the yard. How good it seemed to have Andy as a part of the family! Already he seemed to belong to them all. Who would have guessed the mystery would end this way?

Aunt Jane said, "I'm glad we know the whole story of the woodshed and the potato pit."

"We have had a lot of mysteries," Jessie added. "But this is the first time we ever solved one without Grandfather's help."

Violet nodded. She said, "He will help us with that old letter. I think he might want to put it in a museum."

Benny said, "I think the things ought to be loaned to a school museum. Kids will be interested."

"Yes, that's an idea, Benny," said Henry. "We found the things and you could tell about them. Just like a mystery story."

Andy broke in and said, "No, *I'll* come if you want me, young feller! I like to talk to kids."

"Oh, that will be neat, Andy!" cried Benny. "You know the whole story better than I do."

Henry looked at Jessie. He said, "We could take

pictures of the woodshed and the potato pit. We'd have to take flash pictures. Your John Carter has a wonderful camera, Jessie. Let's ask him to come up here."

Jessie said, "He isn't *my* John Carter, Henry." But Violet looked at her sister's face and saw it turning pink.

"Ask him anyway," said Henry laughing. "He will be here in a minute, I know."

"How do you know?" asked Benny.

"Well, he wanted to stay when he brought Aunt Jane here in the plane. He told me he didn't want to leave. He didn't say why." Henry smiled.

"Well, we still have most of our summer left," said Benny. "I wonder if we will have any more adventures this vacation?"

Aunt Jane laughed. She said, "You will. If Andy is around, there will always be some excitement."

Andy said, "Right, Jane! I'll see to it that you will always have something interesting going on."

"My wedding will be enough excitement for me,

said Aunt Jane. "We'll have to get your grandfather to come up here soon. Maybe Mr. Carter will drive him up."

Everyone heard what she said. But nobody knew what would happen before the summer was over. Not even Aunt Jane herself, nor Andy, nor Henry, nor Grandfather, nor Benny. Not even the man who used to work for the F.B.I.,—John Carter.

About the Author

GERTRUDE CHANDLER WARNER discovered when she was teaching that many readers who like an exciting story could find no books that were both easy and fun to read. She decided to try to meet this need, and her first book, *The Boxcar Children*, quickly proved she had succeeded.

Miss Warner drew on her own experiences to write the mystery. As a child she spent hours watching trains go by on the tracks opposite her family home. She often dreamed about what it would be like to set up housekeeping in a caboose or freight car—the situation the Alden children find themselves in.

When Miss Warner received requests for more adventures involving Henry, Jessie, Violet, and Benny Alden, she began additional stories. In each, she chose a special setting and introduced unusual or eccentric characters who liked the unpredictable.

While the mystery element is central to each of Miss Warner's books, she never thought of them as strictly juvenile mysteries. She liked to stress the Aldens' independence and resourcefulness and their solid New England devotion to using up and making do. The Aldens go about most of their adventures with as little adult supervision as possible—something else that delights young readers.

Miss Warner lived in Putnam, Connecticut, until her death in 1979. During her lifetime, she received hundreds of letters from girls and boys telling her how much they liked her book. And so she continued the Aldens' adventures, writing a total of nineteen books in the Boxcar Children series.